D0458771

TRUCKSGIVING

BY JON SCIESZKA

CHARACTERS AND ENVIRONMENTS DEVELOPED BY THE

DAVID SHANNON LOREN LONG DAVID GORDON

ILLUSTRATION CREW:

Executive Producer:

Creative Supervisor: Nina Rappaport Brown ○ Drawings by: Dan Root ○ Color by: Antonio Reyna

Art Director: Karin Paprocki

READY-TO-ROLL

SIMON SPOTLIGHT
NEW YORK LONDON TORONTO SYDNEY

SIMON SPOTLIGHT
An imprint of Simon & Schuster Children's Publishing Division
1230 Avenue of the Americas, New York, NY 10020

For information about special discounts for bulk purchases, please contact Simon & Schuster Special Sales at 1-866-506-1949 or business@simonandschuster.com. Manufactured in The United States of America 0810 LAK
First Edition 10 9 8 7 6 5 4 3 2 1
Library of Congress Cataloging-in-Publication Data
Scieszka, Jon.
Trucksgiving / by Jon Scieszka ; illustrated by the Design Garage
(David Shannon, Loren Long, David Gordon). – 1st ed.
p. cm. – (Ready-to-read) (Jon Scieszka's Trucktown)
Summary: The trucks of Trucktown create their own annual day of giving thanks.
1. Trucks—Fiction. 2. Thanksgiving Day—Fiction.] I. Shannon, David, ill. II. Long, Loren, ill.
III. Gordon, David, 1965 Jan. 22- ill. IV. Design Garage. V. Title.
PZ7.S41267To 2010
[E]—dc22
2008030031
ISBN 978-1-4169-4146-0 (pbk)
ISBN 978-1-4169-4157-6 (hc)

Many years ago . . .
the first trucks came
to Trucktown.

They scooped dirt.

They dumped dirt.

They mixed cement.

They made roads.

They built Trucktown.

And they saw that it was good.

They wanted a way to say thanks to every truck that helped.

They wanted a way to celebrate every year.

"Let's spray water!"
said the first fire truck.

"Let's smash garbage!"
said the first
garbage truck.

"Ice cream? Ice cream? Ice cream?" said the first ice cream truck.

MAX
MAX
ream

"I've got it,"
said the first Jack.
"Every year we
should have a . . ."

". . . Trucksgiving race!"

And that is just what the trucks do . . .

G

... at this time every year!

HAPPY TRUCKSGIVING!
RITA 1/2